MW00800062

A Gift From

Harford County Public Library

Harford County
Public Library

HCPLonline.org

THE WERE-WOOF

TAKE ANOTHER TRIP TO
SHIVER-BY-THE-SEA:

1: BELLA AND THE VAMPIRE

ERIN DIONNE

ILLUSTRATED BY
JENN HARNEY

PIXEL✦INK

PIXEL❖INK

Text copyright © 2023 by Erin Dionne
All illustrations copyright © 2023 by TGM Development Corp.
Jacket and interior illustrations by Jenn Harney
Excerpt from Shiver-by-the-Sea 3: *The Creature from the Gloppy Green Pool* copyright © 2023 by Erin Dionne
All rights reserved

Pixel+Ink is an imprint of TGM Development Corp.
www.pixelandinkbooks.com
Printed and bound in June 2023 at Maple Press, York, PA, U.S.A.
Series book design by Kerry Martin
Interior book design by Jessica Nevins

Library of Congress Cataloging-in-Publication Data

Names: Dionne, Erin, 1975- author. | Harney, Jenn, illustrator.
Title: The were-woof / Erin Dionne ; illustrated by Jenn
Harney. | Description: First edition. | New York : Pixel+Ink, 2023.
Series: Shiver-by-the-sea ; book 2 | Audience: Ages 7–9. | Audience:
Grades 2-3. | Summary: Bella and her friends discover the real
reason her foster puppy has so much energy.
Identifiers: LCCN 2023018552 | ISBN 9781645951704 (hardback)
Subjects: CYAC: Foster care of animals–Fiction.
Dogs–Fiction. | Werewolves–Fiction.
Classification: LCC PZ7.D6216 We 2023 | DDC [Fic]–dc23
LC record available at https://lccn.loc.gov/2023018552

Hardcover ISBN: 978-1-64595-170-4
E-book ISBN: 978-1-64595-171-1

First Edition

1 3 5 7 9 10 8 6 4 2

For Grafton, who was the Best Dog Ever
—E.D.

For Rosie. A real life "Five"
—J.H.

CONTENTS

CHAPTER 1

An Almost-Full Moon

THE moon was an almost-perfect disc, sending silver light on the wooded road below. A lone figure walked quickly, shoulders hunched, head down, footsteps tapping on the pavement.

Deep in the trees, something rustled. Something *big*.

The figure stopped, turning its head toward the sound.

The rustle came again. Closer this time. A branch snapped. Leaves crunched.

The figure waited. Listened.

More rustling.

Then, deep in the darkness, between the trees: a pair of golden eyes glinted in the moonlight.

A *grrrr-rrrr-rrrrr* rumbled from the figure. It grasped something around its neck.

The eyes disappeared. Branches snapped as heavy footsteps raced away, farther into the woods.

The figure threw its head back. "*Arrrhhh-wooooooo!*" it howled again, triumphant. Then it kept walking.

CHAPTER 2

An Ear-Ringing Howl

BIG balloon arches and fluttering blue, silver, and white flags decorated the Shiver-by-the-Sea town common for Community Day. Tents and tables from local businesses and community organizations dotted the grass, and people milled around, chatting, sampling tiny taquitos from Chiles-by-the-Sea, and enjoying the bright sunny afternoon. The flowers seemed to enjoy it, too, with the hydrangeas showing off their extra-late-season purple and blue blossoms.

The flowers probably are *enjoying themselves*, Bella Gosi thought, snagging her second taquito taster and weaving through the tables on her way across the common. Shiver-by-the-Sea was a magical place—a slightly rusty magical place, according to her mom, but magical nonetheless— and this rusty magical place always surprised her. For instance, lately, there was never any traffic in town. And her magician uncle's tricks weren't tricks at all. And today, though it was supposed to rain, the clouds seemed to stream around the town, not over it.

Bella crossed the street, headed for the corner of one of Main Street's empty storefronts. It was the same spot where she always met her friend Cooper Chaney, and his droopy-eared dog, Casper.

Casper's happy *woof!* reached her ears before they even turned the corner.

"He smelled you," Cooper said.

Bella crouched and scratched Casper's long, velvety ears. He wagged his whiplike tail and nudged her pocket.

"It wasn't me he smelled," she said, standing. She pulled a crumpled bag of pickle 'n' pepper-flavored

potato chips from her pocket. Casper sat and watched her with hopeful eyes. "Just crumbs, buddy." She held the bag out to him. He stuck his nose in and sighed, snuffling up the bits.

"What are we doing today, exactly?" Cooper

asked, eyes on Casper as he searched for chip crumbs on the sidewalk.

"My mom wants us to pass out some flyers, I think."

"Is Bram going to be there?" Cooper asked as he tightened his grip on Casper's leash and the three headed toward the common.

Bella shook her head. Their friend, Bram Orlok, was a vampire. His whole family were, actually. But luckily, instead of being drink-your-blood vampires, they drank syrup and made the most delicious candy anyone in Shiver-by-the-Sea had ever had.

"The Orloks are away at a candy convention. Besides, you know how thirsty he gets on sunny days."

Cooper nodded. "Yeah. He needs so much syrup that he gets . . . sticky."

Bella pointed toward the big Cinema Gosi poster. "There's our table!"

But as the words left her mouth, Casper plopped down right where they were and let out an ear-ringing howl.

CHAPTER 3

A Nap or a Question

"**C**ASPER!" Cooper hissed, tugging on his leash. Everyone in the square—everyone in town, it seemed—stopped what they were doing and turned to stare at them. Bella's face got hot.

Arrrrrrooooooo! Casper let loose again, his long brown and white body trembling. *Was he scared?*

"Stop it!" Cooper commanded while Bella frantically looked around to see what was making the dog so upset. The one other time Casper had made that noise was when they'd found Bram's family. Were there vampires nearby? *Or,* she fretted, *something else?*

Casper took another breath and Bella followed his line of sight.

There.

At their end of the square was one of those shade tents, and under it was a fenced area. A banner hanging from the top read PICK UP YOUR DOG DAY!

The animal shelter, Bella thought. *Of course.*

"It's a whole bunch of dogs from the animal shelter," she explained, relieved that it wasn't some new sort of strange Shiver-by-the-Sea magical monster. "Maybe he wants to play?"

Cooper knelt, trying to get Casper to look at him instead of in the direction of the puppy play area. Thankfully, the distraction worked. The howling stopped.

"He's never done this around other dogs. I'm going to take him that way," Cooper said, pointing away from the puppy tent. "We'll meet you at your mom's table." He tugged the leash and Casper followed as though he'd never let out a peep.

Bella headed to the Cinema Gosi table.

"Check us out, and come by the Sweet Tooth for yummy treats!" her mom said to a woman, handing her a flyer listing upcoming movies. The woman smiled and took a foil-wrapped chocolate, one of Bram's family's specialties.

"How's it going?" Bella asked. Her mom gave her a kiss on the top of her head.

"Meeting lots of people. And the choc-drops are a hit, as always," she said, gesturing to the jar of brightly wrapped treats. "I don't know what the Orloks put in there, but those chocolates are divine."

"Cooper and Casper are on their way," Bella said. "What do you want us to do?"

"I heard them arrive," her mom said with a laugh. "I think everyone did."

Bella flushed again.

"How about you guys do a loop and give out invitations to our Main Street Meets group to the other vendors?" Bella's mom had founded the group shortly after arriving in Shiver-by-the-Sea as part of her plan to get local businesses to rent the empty storefronts in town.

Bella took the square cards, then popped a chocolate in her mouth. She grabbed a few more pieces—she had to share with Cooper, of course—and searched for his blue baseball cap in the crowd.

She spotted him—she couldn't believe it—near the animal shelter table, and moved closer.

A portable pen fenced in about a dozen roly-poly puppies. Brown ones with floppy ears, white fluffy ones, spotted ones . . . They squirmed and nipped and barked and made Bella's cuteness meter explode. And it appeared she wasn't alone. People lined the edge of their fenced-off play area, cooing and squealing.

"Hey, there," she said, finding a space next to Cooper at the edge of the pen.

"Look," he said, pointing at one of the dogs.

It was easily the smallest in the enclosure. The gray and brown bundle of fur was about the size of a piece of paper, curled with nose on paws, tail wrapped around its body, sound asleep as far away from the other puppies as possible.

"Awwww," replied Bella. "What a cutie!"

Cooper furrowed his brow. "Yeah, it's cute, but isn't it a little strange that the other puppies aren't playing with it?"

Bella knew a lot about animals, but she'd never had a dog. "There's a lot happening," she said slowly,

watching a fluffy white pup pounce on a black-and-white spotted one with a short tail. "The other dogs probably don't even notice that that one's asleep. Besides, there's plenty of other friends to play with." She giggled as the dogs rolled and wrestled. She wished she could take them all home.

"Maybe," Cooper said slowly, "but maybe that's why Casper was howling earlier? Maybe he senses something strange about that puppy."

Bella glanced down at Casper, who was snoozing in the grass at Cooper's feet, completely unconcerned with the dogs in the pen. "And *maybe* it doesn't have anything to do with them at all? Last time Casper made that noise, it was because he smelled pickle 'n' pepper potato chips in the Orloks' old store."

Cooper frowned, but before he could say anything, a frizzy-haired woman staring at a clipboard approached the pair.

"Are you here to pick up a puppy?"

The friends shook their heads. "Nope. I'm all set, Ms. Grafton," Cooper answered.

The woman glanced up from the clipboard and dropped her reading glasses low on her nose. "Cooper Chaney! It's you. And Casper." She bent and scratched the basset hound behind his ears. Casper opened one eye and thumped his tail appreciatively.

"Checking out the pups?" she asked, then yawned and rubbed her eyes behind her glasses.

Cooper nodded and introduced Bella. "This is Ms. Grafton. She helped us adopt Casper."

Ms. Grafton perked up, like that reminded her of something. "Can you two come back later?" she said, stifling another yawn. "I want to ask you a question, but I need to get these pups squared away first."

"Sure," Cooper said. "We have to help Bella's mom now, anyway."

The words were barely out of his mouth before Ms. Grafton jetted off to tend to puppies and people.

Cooper nudged Casper awake, and Bella took one last look at the playful puppies.

As they left the tent, Bella explained what they needed to do with the invitations. "Let's go around together?"

Cooper adjusted his baseball cap. "I wonder what she wants to talk to us about?"

"Maybe about getting a nap?" Bella joked. "She seemed awfully tired."

Cooper laughed.

But as they crossed the common, Bella felt a prickle of unease. She glanced behind her. The gray and brown pup was awake, its yellow eyes on her.

And it was still all alone in the enclosure.

CHAPTER 4

Earl's Pet Supplies

BELLA, Cooper, and Casper had nearly finished their lap around the square distributing invitations and chatting. Many of the vendors were handing out free items to promote their businesses, and so far, Bella had picked up a frisbee, a tote bag, and more candy (none of it as good as the Sweet Tooth's).

The last business had a small sign taped to the front of the plain white table that read EARL'S PET SUPPLIES. Colorful collars, individually wrapped dog treats, toys, and other pet needs covered its surface. A half-eaten hamburger, the meat *very* rare, sat on a wrapper off to the side. The owner had their back to them.

"Excuse me?" Bella said quietly, and the person jumped and turned.

The man was tall, with warm brown skin, wide shoulders, a scruff of a beard, and bright green eyes ringed in silver that immediately went to the ground. He didn't say anything.

"Whoa!" Cooper called as Casper pushed past Bella and lunged under the table, straight for the man's legs. "Casper, stop! He must want that burger," he directed to Bella.

The man dropped to the ground. "Hey, buddy. What's your name?" he said, giving Casper scratches behind his ears, exactly where he liked them the most. The dog made a happy noise.

"That's Casper," Bella said. She spoke a little louder, since the man was basically on the ground.

"Casper's a good boy." The man looked up. "I'm Earl."

Bella waited a moment, expecting him to stand, but when he didn't, she glanced at Cooper, who shrugged. "Hi, Earl. I'm Bella, and this is Cooper.

We're dropping off invitations to Shiver-by-the-Sea's new Main Street Meets group for business owners."

"I don't have a business on Main Street," Earl said with a sigh. Casper gave another happy groan and rolled onto his back, showing his belly for rubs. Cooper dropped Casper's leash so he wouldn't get tangled. "I just sell my stuff at markets like this."

A thick silver rope around his neck flashed in the sun as it caught the light. Earl stopped petting the dog to tuck the necklace under his T-shirt. Casper, clearly wondering why the attention stopped, gave him a baleful look.

"Oh," Bella said. "Okay. Well, you could probably still go if you want to. I'll leave the info on your table." She placed the card on a back corner, tucking it under a collar so it wouldn't blow away.

"Sometimes I like animals more than people," Earl said softly.

Cooper smiled. "They're pretty great."

But no sooner had the words come out of his mouth than Casper flipped over and leapt up like someone nearby had opened a bag of pickle 'n' pepper potato chips. Earl rocked back on his heels trying to grab the end of the leash, but the basset hound rocketed away from the table on his short legs letting out big, *booowf*-sounding barks.

"Oh no! Casper! Stop!" Cooper called.

But the dog had already disappeared into the crowd.

CHAPTER 5

A Tiny Puppy?

BELLA and Cooper took off after Casper. Luckily his big, braying barks and all the people jumping out of the way made it easy to follow him. Cooper raced ahead, the bottoms of his sneakers flashing as he sprinted after his dog.

Bella really hoped Casper wouldn't run into the street—

And then came the *Arrrrrooooooooooo!*

Bella, panting, pushed through a crowd gathered in the square and spotted her friend and his dog near the puppy pen. Casper stood howling and howling at the fence while the other dogs, looking confused or scared, had backed up to the far end of the pen. The tiny, gray-and-brown scraggly puppy sat on her haunches in the middle of the enclosure, whimpering at Casper. Her little body shook.

Cooper crouched and grabbed the leash. "Stop it, Casper!"

Arrrrrrooooooo! The sound made Bella's ears ache and her heart pound. The dog was upset . . . because of a tiny puppy?

I guess Cooper was right, she thought. *Casper thinks there's something up with that little floof of a dog.*

Everyone near the shelter pen stared at Casper. A few frowned. Cooper looked like he might cry.

Just then, pet-supply Earl rushed over. He dropped to his knees on the other side of Casper, lifted one of the hound's long brown ears, and whispered something into it.

Arrrooo—ugh!

It was like flicking a switch. Casper's howling stopped and he turned toward Earl, wagging his tail. Earl rubbed behind the dog's ears, gently turning Casper away from the puppy pen.

"How did you do that?" Cooper asked, his voice hushed. "That was amazing."

Earl shrugged, not meeting Cooper's eyes. "I just knew what he needed."

"But he's *my* dog. You just met him. How could you know that?"

Earl finally stood. He brushed at the front of his pants, which were dotted with long dog hairs, then shrugged again, meeting Bella's and Cooper's gazes for the first time. The silver rings around his eyes seemed to glint. "I listened to what he needed. He was scared." Earl nodded toward the tiny pup. "Of that one, apparently."

Cooper shook his head. Bella was amazed. She glanced at the puppy pen. The little dog was curled up again, nose on paws, watching everything with its big golden-brown eyes.

The animal shelter lady, Ms. Grafton, approached them. She looked frazzled, her hair flying everywhere, dark circles under her eyes. "That dog . . . ," she said, glancing over at the gray puppy. "She's so much trouble. I've got pickups pending for all the others, but not that one. I think she needs something more."

"Like . . . a foster home?" Cooper asked.

"Exactly!" Ms. Grafton replied a little too eagerly. "That's what I wanted to ask you about earlier. You wouldn't be able to foster her for a couple of days, would you? You're so good with Casper."

"Me? No way." He laughed. "My dog freaks out around her, and you know I have a bunch of brothers. Besides, we're going to my grandparents' tomorrow. I can't bring another dog home."

"Just for the weekend," Ms. Grafton pleaded. "I really think she could use some time away from the shelter." The shelter lady sounded kind of desperate.

Bella turned to ask Earl if he'd be interested. He seemed like the perfect person to take care of the tiny puppy. But he was already gone.

"What about you?" Ms. Grafton asked, turning to Bella.

"Me?"

CHAPTER 6

Just for the Weekend

BELLA loved animals but had never been able to have a pet in her old apartment in New York City. Instead, she and her dad volunteered at an animal sanctuary together. Now she had no idea what would be allowed in Uncle Van's house . . . especially since she'd hidden a Bram-bat in her room a few weeks ago.

"I just . . . need some rest," Ms. Grafton explained. Bella didn't see what that had to do with the tiny puppy, but maybe running an animal shelter was more exhausting than she realized.

"Just for the weekend?" Bella asked slowly. The puppy *was* awfully cute. . . .

Ms. Grafton nodded. "Yes! Just for the weekend."

She turned to Cooper. "Can you vouch for her? Will she take good care of the puppy?"

Cooper seemed surprised by the question. "Um, yeah. Of course she will. My family had to fill out an application and answer a bunch of questions. Does Bella need to do that, too?"

"Not for the weekend," Ms. Grafton said cheerfully. The relieved expression on her face would have been funny if it didn't make Bella so uneasy.

But it's just for the weekend. What's to worry about? It'll be fun.

"Let me ask my mom," Bella finally said. Cooper raised his eyebrows.

"Great, great! Where is she?" Ms. Grafton peered over Bella's head, as though her mom would suddenly appear.

"Um . . . she runs Cinema Gosi," Bella explained. "She's at her table. I'll go talk to her now."

For a moment, Ms. Grafton's face fell, like Bella had already come back with a no, but she gave Bella a big, fake smile. "Go on, then. We'll be right here!"

Cooper tugged Casper's leash, and they headed in the direction of the cinema table.

"This whole thing was strange," Cooper said. "I'm not sure you should foster that puppy, Bella."

"It was totally strange," she agreed, "but the puppy is so tiny. How could it cause any real trouble?" Even as the words left her mouth, she knew something wasn't right.

"Heard Casper having a bit of a yell again," Bella's mom said when they reached the table. She held out her hand for the remaining Main Street Meets invites.

"Yeah," Bella replied, glancing at Cooper. "He got freaked out by a puppy at the animal shelter tent."

"But Earl, this pet-supply guy, really helped him out," Cooper added. As if Casper knew they were talking about him, he gave a woof and a tail wag.

"Earl?" Bella's mom mused. "Who's that? I don't know anyone named Earl who has a pet-supply business in Shiver-by-the-Sea."

"He doesn't have a shop," Bella explained. "But he

was really good with Casper, and he had all kinds of cool pet things."

"Speaking of pets," Cooper said, nudging Bella, "Bella has something to ask you."

Bella frowned at him.

Ms. Blackstone crossed her arms. "Oh?"

Bella swallowed hard. She wasn't sure she wanted to ask her mom, but she'd promised she would. "The animal shelter lady, Ms. Grafton, asked Cooper if he could foster a puppy for the weekend, and he said he couldn't," Bella began.

"My parents would never let me with my brothers and Casper and everything," Cooper added. "Plus, we're going away."

"So then she asked if I could do it," Bella said in a hurry. "It's a tiny pup, and she seemed pretty sleepy, but I know it's Uncle Van's house and I wasn't sure if it was a good idea—"

"Just for the weekend?" her mom asked.

"Just for the weekend," Cooper confirmed with a nod. "Ms. Grafton said she needed to rest or something."

"You don't have—" Bella said.

"I think that would be fine," her mom said. "You should do it."

CHAPTER 7

What Could Possibly Go Wrong?

"**W**HAT?" Bella and Cooper said at the same time.

"Sure," Bella's mom said. "Look, honey, I know you've missed going to the wildlife sanctuary with your dad, and you've helped me so much with the theater. . . . You've earned a reward and some time with an animal. This seems perfect."

Bella couldn't quite believe what she was hearing. "But what about Uncle Van? Will he be okay with it?"

"He's always saying it's our house, too. And he's coming home from Vegas tomorrow night, so he'll only be there with the puppy one night. I'll text him. I'm sure he'll say it's fine."

Bella, who hadn't wanted to let herself get excited by the possibility, felt a little thrill of hope.

"But you're responsible for it, okay?" Mom said. "And you understand what 'foster' means, right?"

Bella nodded. "If I foster the dog, it means it stays with us for a little while, and then it goes to its forever home or back to the shelter. We aren't going to keep it."

"Exactly," Mom said. "No matter how much you fall in love with her. I'll walk over to the shelter table now and talk with Ms. Grafton, so she knows you have my permission."

Cooper raised his eyebrows at Bella when her mom left. "I know you know about bats and other wild animals, but do you know anything about dogs?"

Bella, who *did* know about bats and owls and raccoons and other creatures, did not really know how to take care of a dog. "A little," she admitted. "I know they need to go for walks and go outside. And they need food and water, of course."

"And you need to play with them. But a puppy's different. Casper is five now, and we got him when I was five. Puppies have a lot of energy. They chew things they aren't supposed to—shoes, blankets, toys—and sometimes they go to the bathroom in the house. Casper ate my whole set of *MonsterTown* action figures when I was six. I was so mad! But I'd left them all over the floor. And he didn't know any better." Cooper glanced down at Casper, who gave him an apologetic look as if to say *That was a long time ago, buddy.*

Bella frowned. She knew puppies did all of those things, but that tiny gray puppy? She was so small and cute and sleepy. It seemed impossible. "I wish you were going to be here to help."

Cooper sighed. "Me too."

"I'll be okay," Bella said after a moment. Right then, she had a heart pang and wished her dad was here with her instead of back in New York. He *loved* animals—all of them, but especially dogs. He'd be so excited to hear that Bella was fostering a puppy! She'd have to send him lots of pictures.

"Of course you will. It'll be great," Cooper said. He reached down and patted Casper on the head. "And besides, it's only for two nights."

"Right," Bella said, feeling better. "Just two nights."

A few minutes later, her mom approached the table carrying a square box alongside Ms. Grafton, who had a reusable shopping bag slung over her shoulder.

"Here you go!" Ms. Grafton said, plopping down the bag. "Everything you need for the weekend. I'm so grateful, Bella."

"And here's our guest!" Mom added.

Bella peered over the edge of the box. The little gray puppy lay curled on a blanket, sound asleep. Squeaky toys, a leash, and some food were jumbled inside the bag.

"Does she have a name?" Ms. Blackstone asked.

"Oh! Well, we let the new owners officially name them, but while they're at the shelter we give them

temporary names based on themes. The most recent batch of pups was named using numbers. So we call this busy girl 'Five.'"

"Perfect." Bella gave Ms. Grafton a bright smile.

What could possibly go wrong?

CHAPTER 8

Golden Rings, Wiry Fur

AFTER Cooper and Casper went home for dinner, Bella helped her mom pack up the table. Five slept soundly in her box, the way she had most of the day. Were puppies nocturnal? Bella didn't think so, but this one slept an awful lot.

When they'd put almost everything away, Bella spotted Earl carrying a plastic storage bin across the common. "Earl! Earl!" she called. The man jumped, then turned. Bella waved at him. "That's the pet-supply guy." Her mom smiled and waved, too.

Earl changed direction and came over to their table, box and all.

"Earl, this is my mom," said Bella. "I'm fostering that little puppy this weekend!"

He gave her a shy smile and nodded at her mom. The adults started talking about his pet supplies.

"There's lots of available space on Main Street."

Bella tuned them out as she peeked into the box. The puppy was still asleep.

That tickle of unease was back.

She's had a busy day. I'm kind of tired, too.

Bella tuned back in to her mom's conversation and heard her mom ask, "Will you come and check out the space tomorrow?"

Earl nodded. "That sounds good."

After they set a time, Earl picked up his box. "It was nice to meet you," he said to both Bella and her mom, then smiled.

As he left, Bella noticed her mom had her Thinking Face on. "If he takes the spot on the corner–the one that used to be the hair salon–he could keep the sinks and do grooming."

Bella shook her head. "You're always trying to get people back into Shiver-by-the-Sea. It's like it's all you think about."

Mom turned to her, serious. "I *do* think about it a lot. If people don't live and work in Shiver-by-the-Sea, the magic will fade. Or worse."

"Worse?" Bella asked, but her mom had turned away to talk with the town librarian.

Bella knew that Shiver-by-the-Sea's magic was rusty . . . but since she'd never even believed that magic was really real until she came to live in the town, she wasn't sure what the difference was between "regular" magic and rusty magic. Uncle Van could already make things appear out of thin air, cause small objects to float across a room, and grow amazing roses. What more could he do if the magic were in full force? And what did her mom mean by "or worse"?

Bella wanted to ask a million more questions, but just then, a snuffling sound came from the box. The puppy stretched, then looked at Bella with big brown eyes rimmed with gold, and wagged her tail.

"Do you want to come out?" Bella asked

gently. She thought Five might have to go to the bathroom.

She grabbed the leash from the shopping bag, then reached in to clip it to Five's collar, but the little dog trembled as Bella got close. "I'm not going to hurt you, sweetie," she said. "It's okay." She kept speaking in a soothing voice as she attached the leash, then gently scooped her up. The small, gray-and-brown dog was warm, and her fur was wiry, so different from Casper's sleek, soft coat. Bella hadn't expected that. And she was light! Bella was certain the little bit of a thing couldn't weigh more than a couple of pounds.

She placed the puppy on the grass, and she obediently walked to the fire hydrant and did her business.

I got this, Bella thought, her shoulders relaxing. *Two nights. I got this.*

CHAPTER 9

Lukewarm Slices

BACK at home, the puppy snoozed peacefully in the cardboard box. Bella's mom said she'd take the leftover materials from the Cinema Gosi table to the theater the next day. "I'm beat," she said. "I'm thinking pizza, a bubble bath, and bed for me."

"Sounds good," Bella said. She went to tuck the puppy box into a corner of the kitchen, but the box seemed . . . *heavier* than it had earlier.

Huh? Maybe something had fallen in? She peered inside. Nope. Just the puppy. But was Bella imagining things, or did it seem bigger?

Puppies grow awfully fast, she thought. But that uneasiness she'd felt on the common crept back in.

"Does Five look different to you?"

Her mom glanced into the box. "She looks okay

to me," she said, then grabbed her phone to order dinner.

When the pizza arrived, the smell of pepperoni, cheese, and sauce made Bella's stomach rumble. The puppy also appeared to like the spicy smell of pepperoni pizza, because she yipped and yipped.

Bella was dying to grab a slice, but taking care of the puppy came first. Before she could cross the room to get the dog, Five had hopped right out of her box. She was *definitely* bigger.

Bella picked her up and lugged her outside, grabbing the leash on the way. She didn't want the puppy to do her business on any of Uncle Van's flowers, so she took her to a back corner of the garden, near the fence.

When they got inside, her mom had blocked the door leading from the kitchen to the rest of the house with a chair and the box so the puppy couldn't run off unsupervised. As soon as Bella put Five down, the puppy went straight to the water bowl and slurped.

"Someone's thirsty!" Mom said. She'd put slices of pizza on plates for each of them.

Bella washed her hands, ready to dive in.

She sat and was about to take a bite of the hot, garlicky pizza when she felt little paws on her leg. She looked down.

The puppy stood on her hind legs, head cocked, staring at Bella with her big, golden-ringed brown eyes, and whined.

"I think she wants dinner, too," Mom said, then took a big bite of her slice.

Bella sighed. Her mom was probably right. Dinner would have to wait.

She carefully moved the pup from her leg, back to all fours, and slid away from the table. Was Five's head closer to her knee then it had been earlier? And were her ears a little less floppy? Bella shook her head as if to clear it. *I'm so hungry I'm imagining things.* "Let's feed you, too," she said.

Bella reached for the note Ms. Grafton had given her with puppy instructions:

One scoop of food + water for breakfast, lunch, and dinner

There was a small scooper in the bin, and Bella used it to measure kibble into Five's dish. Then she added a little water, swished it around, and as a treat, stuck a slice of pepperoni from the now-cooling pizza on top.

"Here you go, sweetie," she said, putting the bowl down. Five raced to it, and Bella returned to her lukewarm slices. She sighed.

"She sure is cute," her mom said.

"She is," Bella grumbled, frustrated that her pizza was cold, while her mom was nearly finished with her own slices.

"Remember: she's still a baby. That's why her needs come first."

Bella nodded, her mouth full of lukewarm pizza. Of course she had to take care of the puppy first—but she was doubting that Five was "still a baby." Something was going on with the magically growing dog.

Wait. Is this a Shiver-by-the-Sea magical hap-pening? Bella wondered. *What if Five ends up like that big red puppy and doesn't fit in the house by tomorrow morning?*

Bella glanced over at the puppy, who'd fallen asleep on the rug in front of the sink.

Definitely bigger.

Mom put the last plate in the dishwasher. "Okay if I go take that bubble bath? Come get me if you need me."

"Of course. I'll be fine, though," Bella said out loud. But inside, she wasn't so sure.

CHAPTER 10

A Squirming, Leg-Kicking Bundle of Fur

BELLA went into the den to watch an episode of *Moonlight Mysteries*, one of her favorite shows. In this episode, Detective Jasper Mover and his partner, June, were investigating the mysterious appearance of a glowing, golden bear in a small town. Bella got sucked in, and the shadows in the room grew darker. Was the golden bear a ghost? She clutched Uncle Van's blanket tight.

Scritch-scritch-thump!

Bella jumped at the sound. On TV, June shouted, "It really *is* a ghost!" Bella's heart went into her throat. She reached over to turn on the light, and a scrabbling sound came from kitchen.

Oh! Of course! The puppy!

Relieved, Bella crossed the room and went to the door. Five had pushed against the box, moving it just enough to leave a tiny opening between it and the chair . . . and she'd squeezed through.

Bella's stomach dropped. *Oh no. Where's the dog?*

"Come here, sweetie!" she called softly, trying to keep calm. "C'mon, Five."

Bella dropped to her hands and knees, peering around at puppy level. Uncle Van had a lot of stuff in his house, which meant a lot of places for a tiny-but-growing puppy to hide. She crawled on all fours, looking under chairs, around tables, and behind magician's trunks.

No puppy. *What if Five is magical? Could she have disappeared?*

Bella stood still, listening hard.

Chuff-chuff-trrrrrrrrrrrrpppp!

There!

She squeezed behind a peacock-blue over-

stuffed chair and spotted a pair of hind legs and a tail swinging back and forth. Bella grasped Five around the waist and slid her out from under the chair. A bright blue piece of fabric came with her!

"That's naughty!" Bella scolded, her heart pounding. *Where's the hole? I hope no one can see it.*

She tucked the puppy—now shaking her fabric-gripping snout wildly from side to side like she'd just won a big prize—under one arm and tilted the chair forward with the other.

The puppy had ripped the fabric under the chair. Bella lifted the puppy so they were nose-to-nose. "You're lucky that no one will see that hole."

The fabric scrap still dangled from Five's mouth. Bella was sure that the puppy was doing her best to grin around it.

"What am I going to do now? Do I tell Mom about the hole?" She frowned at the puppy. Five responded by giving her nose a big, wet lick and letting the fabric scrap flutter to the floor. Bella giggled and tucked Five . . . well, wedged, really—the dog was much bigger than she'd been earlier—under her arm.

She set the blue chair on its legs, hiding the rip. "You need to stay in the kitchen! And . . . you probably need to go out again."

After a quick trip to the yard, Bella put Five down, unclipped the leash, then closed her eyes and raised her arms over her head. Stretching after all that bending and crouching felt good.

Puppy nails skittered across the kitchen floor. Bella assumed Five was racing for more water, but when she opened her eyes, the pup wasn't at the bowl. She wasn't even in the kitchen.

Bella glanced over at the door and groaned. She'd forgotten to block it.

"No, puppy!"

But this time, when she ran into the den, the puppy wasn't trying to hide. Instead, Five was rocketing around the room like she was being chased by a bear—zooming across the floor, up onto an ottoman, jumping to the blue chair, racing across the

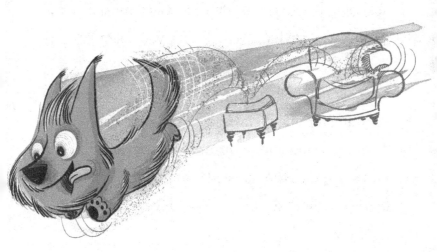

arm, leaping to the couch, diving to the floor. And then she did the lap again. It made Bella dizzy!

"Hey! Five!" she called, wishing the pup would listen. "Stop! Come here!" Bella dove at the ottoman, trying to catch the puppy, but Five seemed to think Bella's racing after her was part of the game, and that made her go even faster. So Bella tried harder. After almost knocking over two lamps and a vase, Bella stopped, breathing heavily.

This isn't working!

The gray ball of fur buzzed around the room for another few seconds, then slowed and stopped, scanning the space for Bella. It was almost as if the puppy was saying, "Why aren't you following me anymore?"

"Gotcha!" Bella said, grabbing her. "That's enough zooming for one night! You can't be out here."

She lugged the squirming puppy back to the kitchen. It *was* the safest place for her, if Bella could find something sturdier to keep Five contained. The puppy whined to get down.

"Oh, no way!" Bella said. "If I put you down before I figure out how to keep you in here safely, there's no telling where you'll end up!"

The puppy was no longer the cuddly fuzzball she'd been cooing over all day. Now she was a much bigger, squirming, leg-kicking bundle of fur that was nearly impossible to manage.

Both of Five's ears stood straight, pointed at the ceiling. They'd been floppy this afternoon, Bella was sure of it. The dog was changing. Fast.

Had Five gotten into some of Uncle Van's magician's materials when she was on her spree in the den?

Whooo-hooooo-hoooo!

Bella jumped, almost dropping the dog. The howl went through Bella's eardrums like an icy needle. "Whoa!"

The puppy craned her neck to look into Bella's face. Her expression was almost like a challenge: *If you don't put me down, I'll do it again.*

Mom's muffled voice called out from upstairs. "Bella, you okay?"

"Fine, Mom," she yelled back through gritted teeth. "Just fine."

CHAPTER 11

She's Just Lonely

BELLA checked her work: heavy books, an otto-man, and a kitchen chair blocked the door leading from the kitchen to the rest of the house. There was no way a tiny puppy could move all of that—any of it—and get loose.

But she's not nearly as tiny as she was, is she?

The dog barreled around the kitchen like she was on a school track, her legs pumping, pointy ears angled back, tail straight out behind her. She easily leapt over a folded-up step stool.

"You're making me tired just looking at you!" Bella complained. *Maybe it's all that napping? Mental note: do not let the dog nap tomorrow.*

As Five raced by again, Bella stifled a yawn. "I've

gotta go to bed soon," she said. It had been a long day. And *she* hadn't napped at all.

But as she plotted how to leave the kitchen without the puppy escaping again, she realized that Five didn't have a bed. She couldn't let her sleep on the kitchen rug all night. *UGH!*

What *did* puppies sleep on?

Something soft, like blankets or towels. There were extra blankets in a trunk in her room. Hopefully she'd find a cozy one for Five in there.

"Stay," Bella ordered. While the dog was busy weaving through the table and chair legs like they were a slalom course, Bella took three running steps and leapt over the new, improved puppy barricade she'd set up in the doorway.

She raced up the stairs that led to her tower room. Just as she put her hand on the doorknob, the sound came again:

Whooo-hooooo-hoooo!

"I'm coming! I'm coming!" she called downstairs in a whisper-yell.

Five evidently didn't hear her, or maybe she didn't care.

Whooo-hooooo-hoooo!

"Bella!" her mom yelled. "*What* is going on?"

"Five's lonely!" Bella called back, bursting into her room and throwing open the chest. "I'm getting a blanket for her bed."

But she wasn't sure if her mom had even heard that last part, because the dog let out another howl, this one even louder.

Whooo-hooooo-hoooo!

She tossed a handmade quilt and some knitted ones onto the floor, grabbed two or three fabric blankets that felt soft and cozy, then ran out without bothering to put the others away.

Whooo-hooooo-hoooo!

"Coming!" she yelled, pounding down the stairs as fast as she could.

The puppy sat on the kitchen side of the barricade, tilting her head back to howl again. Her muzzle was long and streamlined, and did her nose seem more pointy?

"I'm here! I'm here!"

When Five saw Bella, she leapt in a funny circle and spun, chasing her tail. Bella piled the blankets in a corner. "Come on, sweetie. Try out your bed. Aren't you tired?"

Apparently, the dog was *not* at all tired. Not one little bit.

Instead of lying on the bed, she grabbed a corner of it, shaking the blanket and fake-growling. Bella halfheartedly tried to pull it back. The puppy loved this new game, digging in deeper and tugging harder.

Tug-of-war?

Bella gave the blanket a jolt, and the pup yanked, her little legs braced against the floor to stay put. Five was stronger than she looked. Bella gave a few more short tugs, then yawned and glanced at the giant gold and blue peacock fan clock over the

microwave. It was late! No wonder she was so tired.

Five snarled like a full-grown dog, pouncing on a blanket corner.

"That's it! I'm done," Bella announced. "Time for bed—for both of us." She picked up the dog and settled her onto the piled-up blanket.

The puppy wanted nothing to do with bedtime. She took off again, zooming around the kitchen.

"Listen, sweetie. I have to get some sleep. And

that means you do, too." Bella turned off the kitchen lights, but that only seemed to make the little dog run *faster*.

Would this dog ever *get tired?*

Bella couldn't wait around to find out. She inched her way across the kitchen, hoping to sneak away without Five noticing. She carefully stepped over the barricade. . . .

The puppy froze, then tilted her head back.

"Shhhhhh!"

The dog did stop, but she also started running again.

This is not going to work, Bella thought irritably. How was she going to get any sleep?

CHAPTER 12

Like a Cherry on a Yucky Cake

"PLEASE, go to sleep," Bella begged the puppy hours later. She'd brought her out, played more, sat on the kitchen floor (where she'd fallen asleep for a few minutes against the fridge door), and finally, all out of ideas, Bella had clipped the leash to Five's collar and led her up to her room so she could get some rest. She'd tried to carry the dog, but Five had gotten so big and was so heavy, Bella was afraid she'd drop her. All the while, the pup ran and jumped and growled and played and zoomed and . . .

Bella closed her bedroom door and did a quick inspection of her floor, then unclipped the leash.

She piled the mess of blankets on her bed, then climbed on top.

The door was closed. There was nothing Five could break. She could just run until she was–

Boom! Crash!

Bella jolted out of a deep sleep. She sat straight up in bed, unsure as to where she was. This wasn't her room in New York City, with its view of the fire escape. This room had birdcages everywhere, and . . . That's right. She was in her new room. At Uncle Van's.

But what had caused that sound?

And then it all came back to her: the puppy, the running around, the howling . . .

Five!

Bella hopped out of bed, searching for the dog. After peering under her bed, she turned and froze. The bedroom door was open. How had that happened?

Bang!

Bella raced downstairs, realizing when she got to the bottom that she was still wearing her clothes from the day before.

"Hey, sweetie!" she called softly. The sky was the light gray of early morning–definitely too early for her mom to be up. "Come here, girl!"

The cluttered hall was a still life of silver shadows. Delicate fans of peacock and ostrich feathers rose from behind boxy trunks and glittering mirrors. Bella peered into the gloom.

Splish!

Her bare foot came down in something cold and wet. *Water? Why is the floor wet?*

Not water.

Oh gross. Bella hopped toward the kitchen, trying to figure out if she should clean her foot first, or find the puppy and *then* clean her foot. She paused, perched on one leg, propping herself against a sarcophagus-shaped bookcase.

Bump!

Find the puppy, she decided.

She walked on her toes of the wet foot, trying not to track dog pee all through the house. What was making all that noise?

When Bella reached the den, she had her answer: Throw pillows on the floor. Uncle Van's collection of magician's linking rings from around the world flung everywhere.

And a white feather snowstorm swirling above it all.

Feathers?

There were no feathers in the den. The only thing that had any feathers was—

Bella turned to her uncle's big purple chair and gasped. Five had jumped up and pulled Uncle Van's favorite TV blankie to the floor, shredding it and sending its down filling flying.

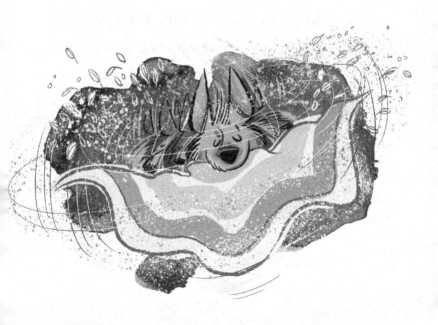

And, to top it off, a pile of dog poop decorated the center of the room like a cherry on a yucky cake.

But where was the puppy?

Bella called her, gently, quietly, trying not to sound upset. That might only scare Five more. "Come on out, honey. I need to see if you're okay." As she searched the room, Bella forgot about her pee-covered foot. She gathered the linking rings, looping them around one arm like oversized bracelets, all the while wondering how she was going to clean up the feathers and hide the rest of the damage. As she reached for an emerald green throw pillow, Bella spotted a fluff of gray fur sticking out from under the side of the couch.

"Gotcha!" she said, pouncing.

But instead of Five the puppy, Bella pulled out a stuffed magician's rabbit.

She tossed it on the couch and raced to the kitchen, sure the little dog would be in there. But

there was no dog, and the back door—which she was sure she'd closed when she brought Five in the last time, hadn't she?—was open a crack.

A crack large enough for a puppy to wiggle through.

Her heart sank.

"Oh no."

CHAPTER 13

Escape Artist

BELLA slipped her smelly pee foot into a pair of her mom's sneakers sitting by the back door and raced into the yard, her heart pounding.

"Five! Come on, girl!" she called and whistled, wishing the puppy had a name she recognized. Her throat was dry with fear. Where could the little puppy be?

The early morning sunshine warmed the heavy dew on the grass, making a low mist in Uncle Van's garden. The bright flowers dripped with water, and every one of his garden statues was a blurry shadow.

Heart pounding, hands sweating, Bella wanted to run around in circles. She didn't know what to do. Then her dad's voice popped into her head: *In an emergency, you need to stay calm in order to be a helper.*

She stopped and tried to breathe through her panic. She needed to find the puppy, but freaking out wouldn't make that happen any faster. Then, she remembered what the wildlife rehabilitator had said on one of her visits: *When you're looking for an injured animal, use your senses. Look around. Listen carefully. Sniff the air for unusual scents.*

Bella closed her eyes and took a deep breath. She smelled the perfume of the flowers, the wet smell of the morning, and dog pee from her foot.

She listened: twittering birds just waking up, calling their friends.

This wasn't helping!

Stay calm, she told herself.

She opened her eyes to really *look*: mist floating along the ground, heavy wet plants bending with dew, a small, trampled path of grass—

That's it!

Five had run through the wet grass, flattening it as she went.

Bella's body buzzed with excitement. "I'm coming, sweetie!" she called.

Keeping her eyes on the path, Bella followed it downhill. Occasionally, the track disappeared into one of the backyard's many flower beds, but the pup had always returned to the lawn after racing around in the dirt.

At the bottom of the hill, right up against the fence in an area of the yard Bella had never even explored, she spotted a pile of dirt.

And a hole, just big enough for a puppy.

One hundred terrible scenarios raced through Bella's mind. Before she could panic again, however, she realized there was a back gate just a few steps away. She unlatched it and raced to the other side of the hole ... in a neighbor's backyard. A neighbor's late-season backyard vegetable garden, to be precise.

And it was a mess. Carrots all over the ground. Clods of dirt everywhere.

And in the middle of the mess: one dirt-covered, snoring puppy.

"Of course," Bella said, sighing. "Of course."

CHAPTER 14

Everything's Fine

BY the time her mom came downstairs for breakfast, Bella had cleaned the puddle and poop, put the room back together, swept up the feathers, and tucked what was left of Uncle Van's blanket into a big shopping bag. She'd even given Five a quick bath in the sink using the spray nozzle to get the dirt off before wiping her dry with an old towel.

She was so tired. Her eyes felt like they had sand in them, her body hurt . . . and the dog had slept through everything but the bath, curling up like a fluffy angel as soon as she was dry.

"How was the rest of the night?" Mom asked as she brewed a pot of coffee. "You look like you didn't sleep well."

Bella drooped at the kitchen table, picking at a

bowl of cereal. She wasn't ready to tell her mom about the disastrous night. And morning. "Fine. The puppy kept me up a little." Bella yawned so big, her ears popped.

"She's just a baby," Mom said, pouring her coffee. "And it's a new place. It's exciting and scary for her."

Bella glanced at Five, snuggled onto the blanket in the corner. The pup was back to her tiny, floppy-eared self. Bella had carried her all the way up the hill from the neighbor's yard. Had she imagined the dog getting bigger last night? Maybe it was because she was so tired that the dog seemed larger and heavier?

Mom was probably right, but Bella didn't feel excited about anything—only grouchy about everything. Well, that wasn't true. *Nervous and a little scared.* She also felt that.

The puppy had basically destroyed Uncle Van's blanket. What would he say when he saw the damage? Would he yell? Tell them that they couldn't stay with him anymore? Bella kind of doubted that— Uncle Van was so kind—but it was his favorite blanket! She'd be upset if she was away and someone ruined something she loved. And it wasn't a regular blanket, where you could just sew up the holes. How do you add feathers back into a blanket?

Plus, Five had dug up the neighbor's garden!

Bella didn't even know who lived back there, and now she'd have to tell them her foster puppy had destroyed their carrots.

She was about to confess the truth, but her mom changed the subject before she could get the courage. "I have to go to the theater this morning to empty that stuff from the car, meet Earl to help him check out the empty storefront, and get ready for tonight's show. Do you want to meet me for lunch?"

Bella nodded, eyeing her mother's cup of coffee. She wasn't allowed to drink it, but knew it would help her stay awake.

"Why don't you take the puppy for a walk?" Mom suggested, going to grab her sneakers. "Have her get some of that energy out."

Bella groaned. Walking the dog meant using energy, too—and all Bella wanted to use was her bed to take a nap. But she only had the puppy for one more night, so . . .

"I'll do that," she said, yawning again.

"Go get ready, and we can leave together." Her

mom furrowed her brow and gave her sneaker a sniff.

Bella slurped another spoonful of soggy cereal, then trudged to the staircase. On her way, she grabbed the bag containing Uncle Van's blanket. *No sense leaving it down here where it could get even more wrecked.*

Not that she was hiding it. . . . She wasn't doing that, not at all.

CHAPTER 15

It's Who She Is

"**COME** on!" Bella snapped. The sleepy puppy was dragging—literally. Five wanted to snooze instead of walk. Bella had tried talking to the dog nicely, nudging her when she lay down. Finally, she resorted to giving the leash periodic tugs to bring the little dog along. She felt bad about it, but how else was she going to keep the pup awake? They'd barely made it past Uncle Van's gate, and they still had to walk all the way down the hill into town.

Ugh!

While Bella stopped to think of a better plan, the dog fell asleep in a sunny patch of sidewalk. Frustrated, Bella bent and scooped the puppy up. This morning she was light enough to carry, and Bella figured *one* of them should get a nap.

The puppy snuggled into the crook of Bella's arm, and she tucked the end of the leash into her pocket. Once they reached the bottom of the hill and got to Main Street, she'd put Five down and wake her up. Again.

She trudged down the hill, thinking about what she was going to do about Uncle Van's blanket and the neighbor's carrots—she'd have to tell her mom about both over lunch—which is why she was so startled when she heard someone say her name.

"Hi, Bella!"

She looked around. Who was calling her? She spotted someone across the street, waving. At first, Bella didn't recognize the woman, and all her flags went up. Who was she? What did she want?

Then, as the woman crossed the street, Bella realized it was Ms. Grafton, from the animal shelter. Bella hadn't recognized her because she looked so . . . *good*. Less frazzled.

More well-rested.

Then everything clicked. "This dog doesn't sleep. At least, not at night. That's why you asked me to foster her!"

Ms. Grafton nodded, a guilty expression flitting across her face. "I was so tired. You have no idea. I had to sleep at the shelter two nights last week because her howling kept the other dogs up and the neighbors complained. I've never seen anything like it. I brought her in to the vet, thinking there was something wrong with her, but he says she's just 'extra energetic' and needed more playtime." She sighed. "With so many other dogs at the shelter waiting for new homes, I couldn't give even more time to this one. It wasn't right."

Bella was with her all the way up until the *there was something wrong with her.* "I don't

think there's anything *wrong* with Five...," she said slowly, suddenly feeling protective of the wild puppy. "I think it's who she *is*. But it's an awful lot," she added miserably. "And you should have told me. You know, you kind of tricked me!"

The woman flushed. "I'm sorry, Bella. I was so tired. Look, I'll take her back tomorrow. Hopefully, we can find someone to adopt her. But I just need one more good night's sleep."

Bella wanted to hand the puppy over right then and there and make Ms. Grafton take her, but just at that moment, the dog woke up, sighed, and wiggled closer. Bella glanced down into the pup's big, golden-rimmed brown eyes. Five licked Bella, then closed her eyes and went back to sleep.

"Fine," Bella mumbled, her heart melting. "One more night."

Ms. Grafton looked so happy, like she could bounce away. "She'll be fine," she called to Bella. "Nap this afternoon, so you're ready for later!"

That's not much help, Bella thought.

But at the same time, she wasn't sure what her next step should be. She knew no matter what, the dog was going to be up all night.

And so was she.

CHAPTER 16

Hello, Earl

BELLA stopped at the bottom of the hill, unsure where to go or what to do next. She could head over to the theater, but it was still early, and putting boxes away and unpacking the car felt like a lot of work when she was so tired. Maybe she'd try the library and see if the librarians would let the sleepy puppy hang out while she checked out books?

"Hon! What're you doing here?" Her mom's voice made her jump.

"Oh, hey. I'm going to the library. The puppy doesn't want to walk." Bella yawned. "Why aren't you at the theater?"

"I'm meeting the gentleman with the pet-supply business," Mom explained, glancing at her watch.

"He should be here any minute. I got the key to the space from Main Street Meets."

The information slowly moved through Bella's foggy brain, but then she remembered—Earl! She realized they were standing outside of the empty storefront on the corner, where she met Cooper and Casper all the time.

"Hello," came the soft voice. Earl walked along the sidewalk, eyes down, hands in his pockets. "You said to meet you here, right?" he asked hesitantly.

"Yes! Absolutely!" Bella's mom fumbled the key into the door lock.

"Hi, Earl," said Bella, yawning again as her mom got the door open and went inside to turn on the lights.

"Is that your dog now?" Earl asked. He crouched down and gently ran a finger along the puppy's head, managing not to wake her.

The question surprised Bella. At first, she didn't know how to answer, but Earl's face was kind,

and he was so gentle with Five, and she was so tired. . . . "I'm fostering her for the weekend. She stays up all night. She's wild. She zooms around and howls and wrecks things. She even dug up our neighbor's carrots and wrecked my uncle's blanket! She's a totally different dog when the sun goes down. She gets bigger! The shelter lady, Ms. Grafton, even took her to the vet to see if something was wrong with her, but of course there isn't. I just wish she'd calm down and let me *sleep*."

After the rush and tumble of words, she was a little surprised to find that what was left was relief.

Earl looked up sharply, his silver-ringed green eyes meeting hers. "She behaves that way at night?" he asked carefully.

Bella nodded.

"*Only* at night?"

Bella nodded again. "Only at night, at least, that's all I've seen. Well, the carrots were this morning."

Earl frowned and looked at the puppy, then moved away.

"I need to see the store," he said gruffly. Bella stepped back, and he brushed by her, reaching for the door. Was he angry? Had she said something wrong?

Just before he went inside, he turned to face her. "Bring the puppy here this afternoon. We'll see what we can do."

Before Bella could respond, he slipped into the shop, leaving a confused Bella and the sleepy puppy on the sidewalk.

Could Earl help? A carrot-shaped dash of hope sprouted inside her.

She scratched Five's ears. "Maybe we'll solve your mystery, after all," she whispered to the puppy.

CHAPTER 17

Three Parts

AT the sidewalk table at Chiles-by-the-Sea, the town's taqueria, Mom bubbled on and on about Earl and the possibility of his new pet boutique. "The space is small," she said, "and it has a funny shape, but it's perfect for his needs. He was so happy to see the sinks, and he told me he'd never thought of adding grooming services to his business. He's going to take it, Bells!"

Bella smiled at her mom. Having another new business open on Main Street *was* pretty exciting. Plus, she liked Earl, even though he was the shiest adult she'd ever met.

"He's going to help me with the puppy," Bella said. A wave of anxiety crashed through her as she took a sip of her lemonade. "Uncle Van comes back today, doesn't he?" She shifted her gaze, avoiding her mom. Five stirred at her feet, and Bella scooped the puppy up and put her in her lap, where she went back to sleep.

"He's probably back now," Mom said. "Why? What's wrong?"

Bella picked at the edge of her burrito. "I'm happy to see Uncle Van," she said slowly, "but when the puppy got out last night, she made a mess in the den. . . ."

"Which you cleaned up beautifully."

"I didn't tell you that she also shredded Uncle Van's favorite TV blanket." Bella hung her head. "There were feathers everywhere."

"Oh." Mom was quiet for a moment. "You have to tell him and you're worried about that."

"Yeah."

Mom wiped her mouth with her napkin. "Well, those conversations aren't always easy, but your

uncle will understand. And you can use our guide-
lines for offering a good apology, right?"

"Mom!" Bella rolled her eyes. "That's from when
I was a baby!"

Her mom's eyes darkened. "A good apology is *not* just for babies. It's for everyone. What are the three parts?"

Bella squirmed in her chair. The puppy, nestled in her lap, lifted her head, annoyed to be woken up a second time. Bella cleared her throat. "The three parts to a good apology are 'I'm sorry, this is what I did, and this is what I'm going to do to correct it,'" she said, rolling her eyes when her mom joined in on the last part. "But *I* didn't do anything, and I don't know how to correct it."

Mom tilted her head, looking remarkably like the puppy. "You are caring for Five. And that makes her behavior an extension of yours, so you have to take responsibility for her actions. As for how to correct the problem, I'm sure you'll think of something."

"Thanks," Bella said, feeling even more miserable. Her mom was right. And she also knew, deep down, that if she had a nap, she'd probably be better equipped to think about this stuff.

She scooped Five into her arms and stood.

"Do you want to save the rest of these for Casper?" Mom asked, shaking the bag of leftover tortilla chips.

"No thanks," Bella said. "He only likes pickle 'n' pepper flavor. And this little dog doesn't seem to like anything except meat."

"Just like that guy," her mom said, pointing across the street to *The Werewolf* poster hanging outside the theater. "That's this week's show."

"What's that movie about?" Bella joked. "Some regular guy who transforms into a wolf at the full moon?" But even as she said the words out loud, a chill went down her spine. She glanced at the puppy in her arms.

"You're exactly right," her mom said before Bella could get any further with her thoughts. "Unfortunately, in most werewolf movies, there's no happy ending for the wolf. Silver and were-wolves don't go together."

Bella got the idea.

"Yikes! I'm not sure I want to see that, then." As Bella stroked Five's head, her thoughts turned to dogs that magically grew and shrank, full moons, and messy gardens.

CHAPTER 18

Pepperoni

A FEW minutes later, Bella's mom headed to the theater to unpack the car. Bella approached the empty storefront. *Although it won't be that way for much longer*, she thought. She knocked on the dirty glass.

As if they knew change was coming, the husks of the plants in the planters on either side of the door had sprouted green shoots between morning and lunch.

This is Shiver-by-the-Sea. Of course they know.

When Earl opened the door, his shirt and pants were splotched with dust.

"So, you're taking it," Bella said, smiling. Earl gave her a shy grin. The silver circles around his green eyes seemed to glow brighter.

"Sure am. Seems like the right place. In a lot of ways," he added, eyes on the planter. "Shall we take a look at this pup?"

He motioned to a counter, and Bella placed the little dog on top. She stretched, then woke up, looking all around.

Earl petted the puppy, but the dog didn't meet his gaze. "Hey, girl," he coaxed. "Let me see your eyes."

"Do you have a dog?" Bella asked as Five curled up on the counter and went back to sleep.

Earl startled, almost as though he'd forgotten she was there. "No. Most dogs don't . . . take to me. I have a . . . condition . . . that makes them nervous."

"Casper took to you. My friend's dog with the big ears."

Earl nodded. "That's why I'm taking this space," he said. "Things seem kind of different here."

Bella smiled. "Shiver-by-the-Sea is *very* different."

"This pup seems different, too. What wakes her up?"

"Maybe a piece of pepperoni," Bella said, remembering how excited the puppy had been about her pizza the night before.

"Pepperoni, huh?" Earl mused. "Stay right here." He left the store and returned a few minutes later, a small stick of pepperoni in his hand.

He unwrapped it, then waved it in the air in front of the puppy's nose. The dog's eyes immediately opened, the golden rings around the brown irises shining.

"There you go," Earl said, a funny expression on his face as the puppy eagerly gnawed at the end of the stick. "It's what I thought. I have something that can help."

"What is it?" Bella asked. "Does it have something to do with her eyes? I've never seen any that shine like that."

Earl focused on the floor. "Sort of," he mumbled. He handed the stick of pepperoni to Bella. "I have to go to my car," he said, before leaving the store again.

Bella was surprised by his second quick exit. As she stood there, letting the puppy eat the pepperoni, she thought about what Earl had said . . . and that movie poster.

Both he and the puppy had strange circles around their irises, the colored parts of their eyes.

Was it possible they had the same condition? Could dogs and people share a disease?

Bella knew it was possible. At the wildlife rescue, the ranger had told the volunteers that there were a few diseases that passed between animals and humans, but she couldn't think of one that made dogs change behavior at night. Rabies? That would be scary, but puppies got shots for that. Plus, wild animals got rabies more than domestic animals. And it wasn't something humans could catch, unless they were bitten.

She glanced at what was left of the pepperoni. *Bitten*. The dog liked meat. And she changed size and became wild at night. . . . And then the movie poster for *The Werewolf* flashed across her mind.

A werewolf. Five nommed on the pepperoni, giving a happy growl.

Was the dog some kind of werewolf?

And . . . was Earl?

CHAPTER 19

A Werewolf?

By the time Earl came back into the empty store, the pepperoni was gone and Bella was convinced that he and Five shared a wolfish secret. She wasn't scared—yet. Werewolves were night monsters, and it was daytime. Plus, the other monsters she knew— Bram's family, the Orloks—were nice. Earl seemed nice, too. And so did the puppy, when she wasn't running around and wrecking everything.

Earl's shadow appeared at the door. Bella gulped hard, fighting a thread of fear.

"Let's try this," Earl said as he came in.

Bella's face must have showed something about what she was thinking, because he stopped. "Are you okay?"

"Are *you*?" She knew it probably sounded rude,

but it was less rude than asking someone "Are you a werewolf?" Probably. Right?

"I'm fine," Earl said. He kept his eyes lowered. "I think this may help the puppy," he said, placing a collar on the counter. He backed away, then pretended to check something on his phone.

Earl's whole vibe had changed when Bella asked her question. Instead of facing her and meeting her eyes, he'd turned away, gaze to the ground, not connecting with her. It was like he'd sunk back in on himself—and he was a pretty big person to sink so small. Bella's heart cracked with sadness for him. He seemed so lonely.

"Oh, thank you so much," she said, forcing the words to sound cheerful. She picked up a new yellow collar with a shiny tag hanging from it. A *silver* tag.

Just like the silver necklace Earl wore!

In the movies, silver kills werewolves, she thought. *But movies aren't real. Werewolves . . . are?*

Vampires are real, she told herself. *And the ones you know don't drink blood. They make yummy truffles and live here in Shiver-by-the-Sea.*

She sighed. When she examined the collar, Earl glanced up, then quickly went back to scrolling through his phone.

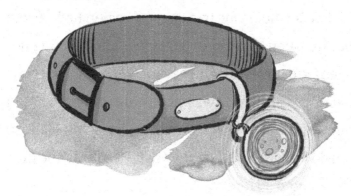

"This won't hurt her, right?" Bella asked. Earl shook his head, and Bella clipped the new collar around the puppy's neck and unhooked her old one. As soon as the new collar clicked into place, the puppy gave a deep sigh and wagged her tail.

"I left space for her name." Earl paused. "Does she have a name?"

Bella shook her head. "The shelter calls her *Five*, but that's not her real name. I think who-ever adopts her should get to name her. And thank you, again, for this. The collar is so pretty, but do you think it can actually help her?" Bella went to scratch Five under her chin, and she gasped. The golden rings around the dog's eyes had turned silver. Like Earl's.

"She'll probably still be up most of the night, but she won't be as . . . busy. You should be able to keep her in your room with some toys and she'll be fine."

Bella took a breath. She had to know. Even if it meant upsetting a grown-up.

"Do you know this because she's a . . . you're some kind of a . . . werewolf?" Saying the word felt like dropping a bomb in the middle of the floor, one that could go off any minute.

"Why do you say that?" Earl asked, an edge to his voice. Was it Bella's imagination, or did his voice sound deeper, too? She took a breath to calm herself.

"It's just . . . it makes sense. The meat, being wild at night, the silver, the . . ." She gulped. "The eyes."

The store was silent, except for the puppy's tail thumping against the table.

"It's a condition," Earl said quietly. "In my family. It makes it hard to live anywhere for long, because I'm different at night. Not dangerous," he added quickly. "Just *different*. The silver helps keep my personality the same, but there are other . . . changes. It keeps them less noticeable so I can be out in the world. I think it should work the same way for the puppy, although I've only seen one other dog with it." His face drooped like he was exhausted, but not like the way Bella felt. Not being able to settle anywhere was probably a whole different type of tired.

"That sounds hard," Bella began. "And maybe kind of lonely. But Shiver-by-the-Sea is a pretty magical place, and there are other . . . types . . . of people here who are a little bit different. But they just make Shiver-by-the-Sea more special. More

magical." She paused, not knowing if she should go on, but Earl's silver-rimmed eyes were on her now. "So . . . so maybe this will be a place you can stay, too?"

Earl was quiet for a few moments, and Bella wondered if she'd said something wrong. He lightly petted the puppy, then turned his attention back to Bella.

"Do you think so? Do you really think I can stay?"

Bella considered her answer. "The longer I've been here, the more I realize it's the people that help Shiver-by-the-Sea's magic grow. I think the town needs you." She smiled.

Earl met her eyes, the silver rings around his irises glowing.

"I think I need it, too."

CHAPTER 20

All Apologies

BELLA felt better as she carried Five home. Earl could breathe a little easier in Shiver-by-the-Sea, and maybe–just maybe–the silver tag would help chill the puppy out, and then she could get some sleep.

But there was no sleeping, and no chilling out, until she took care of a few things:

Uncle Van.

The blanket.

The neighbor's garden.

A rock of dread settled in her stomach, and it got even bigger when she saw her uncle sitting on the front porch swing.

"Hey, best niece ever!" he called.

"Hey, best uncle ever," she replied, though with less enthusiasm. She didn't feel like the Best Niece Ever. She felt like the worst one.

"Whoa, who's that?" he asked as she climbed the stairs.

"She's not staying long," Bella responded.

Her uncle scratched the dog's ears, then patted the cushion next to him. With a snap of his fingers, two big, frosty glasses of lemonade appeared on the table. "I couldn't do *that* when I left for Vegas!" he said, amazed. "Something's going on around here!"

"What did you think was going to appear?" Bella asked, climbing onto the swing and setting Five on her lap.

"Honestly, I was hoping for empty glasses so you could go get the lemonade," he confessed, "but this is even better!"

She took the frosty glass he handed her and sipped. The bright lemonade felt good after her hot walk up the hill.

"It's been a weekend," she said. Bella told him all

about the puppy, the werewolf, Earl, the long night. She stopped and took a breath.

"Last night, she escaped from my room when I finally fell asleep and made a mess downstairs. I cleaned it up. Except . . . she kind of tore your favorite blanket."

Uncle Van whistled. "Did the feathers come out?"

Bella nodded, miserable, but pushed on. "She also got loose and dug up all the carrots in your back neighbor's garden. And she dug a hole under the fence. I'm pretty sure she's a werewolf. Were-dog. Were-woof?" She met Uncle Van's eyes, and they both burst out laughing.

But there was something more she had to do. She remembered the three parts to her apology. "I'm so sorry that I didn't supervise her properly. I'm not sure how to fix your blanket, but I'm going to try. And I need to apologize to the neighbors."

Uncle Van was quiet for a minute. "I could be angry that you and your mom let an overactive werewolf puppy into my house, where it pooped and peed on my floor, dragged the pillows and rings around, and wrecked my favorite blanket. I *could* be totally angry about that."

Bella held her breath, heart pounding. *How much trouble am I in?*

Uncle Van winked at her and rubbed his chin. "Or, instead, I could be happy that your mom felt comfortable making a decision involving the house, that you were responsible in cleaning everything up, and that you told me the truth about what happened and apologized so beautifully. That shows me that you're both feeling comfortable here, and that is what I want. Even if my cuddle blankie gets damaged in the process."

Bella squeezed her uncle's hand. "You are pretty much the best."

"I know. And I think this Pretty Much Definitely the Best Uncle is going to teach you how to sew so you can fix my blanket. And I'll introduce you to Mrs. Lovelace, my neighbor with the garden. She's the town librarian."

Bella nodded. "I'll apologize to her, too. And offer to help fix her yard."

Uncle Van gave her a gentle nudge with his elbow. "Now you're talking."

The puppy gave an extra-loud snore, and they both giggled.

CHAPTER 21

Silver Rings

THE next night, right at dusk, Bella and the puppy waited outside of Cinema Gosi, where people were lining up to see the werewolf movie. Her whole body ached. Not from lack of sleep, but from bending over resetting the carrots that could be replanted, harvesting the ones that couldn't, and straightening the dirt in Mrs. Loveland's garden all afternoon.

"How'd it go?" came a deep voice from behind her. Bella turned. Earl stood there, looking a little . . . bigger . . . than he had the day before. His hair curled around his collar, and his beard looked longer. And were his eyes darker green?

"Great!" Bella said. Five stretched and wagged her tail, looking up happily at Earl. "You were right. The new collar did the trick. She perked up around this time, we played for a bit, and then she behaved herself in my room when I went to sleep. She's like a totally different dog. Oh, and check out her eyes."

The puppy—who was a little bigger, but not as big as the first night Bella had her—raced over to Earl and pounced on his sneakers, grabbing the end of a shoelace in her mouth and tossing her head

from side to side, play-growling. Earl bent to pick her up, and the dog leapt into his arms.

Bella dropped the leash. "She really likes you." The silver rings around the dog's eyes mirrored the ones in Earl's. "You know—"

Just then, Ms. Grafton rushed up to them. "I'm so sorry I'm late," she said, looking even better than she had the day before. Her dark circles had vanished, and she seemed calmer. "I was held up. I hope you got a little bit of rest last night, Bella?"

"Five was a dream."

"She *was*?" Ms. Grafton couldn't hide her astonishment. It made Bella giggle.

"Oh, yeah. There's nothing wrong with Five. You just have to know how to manage her energy," Bella said, winking at Earl, who was still cuddling the puppy. He grinned—a big, wolf-like grin—back at her.

"Well, then," Ms. Grafton said, looking back and forth from Bella to Earl. "It sounds like you really clicked with her."

"Kind of," Bella said. She let a wolfish smile of her own come across her face. "But I have even more exciting news!" The two adults waited. "I think I may have found her a forever home."

Earl froze. Ms. Grafton raised her eyebrows.

The puppy gave Earl a big, slobbery lick.

"You have?" Earl asked. He furrowed his brow, like he wasn't sure Bella had made the right decision. "This pup needs special attention." He put the dog down, as though he was trying put distance between them.

Ms. Grafton shook her head. "You *have*?"

"I think so," said Bella mischievously. "She definitely needs someone special to care for her. Plus, there's a new business opening on Main Street, and I think it needs a mascot. What do you say, Earl?"

His mouth dropped open, revealing some rather large teeth. He snapped it shut, face beaming. "Definitely."

"Well, we have procedures to follow," Ms. Grafton said, "but if you are interested and meet the criteria,

I think this could work out beautifully. I'll need you to come in and fill out paperwork, of course. . . ."

Bella smiled and stepped back, letting the grown-ups discuss the details. She was sure that Ms. Grafton would let Earl adopt the pup.

She crouched and rubbed Five behind the ears. "You be the best girl for Earl, okay?" she whispered. "He needs a friend." The dog gave her a lick. Bella's heart panged with loss, but she knew Earl would take good care of her. "I'll come and visit you at the shop, okay? I'll even bring pepperoni." The little dog's tail whipped back and forth with joy. Bella kissed Five on the head and stood.

I wonder what he'll name the puppy?

"Hey, Bella!"

She spun.

"Sorry I'm late!" Cooper huffed as he ran up to her, like he'd rushed all the way from his house. "We hit traffic on the way back. But—you know, it cleared up right when we got to town."

"How's Nana?"

"Great!" he said. He gestured to a small paper bag looped over his arm. "She sent you a piece of her famous carrot cake! What's the movie tonight?"

"*The Werewolf*," Bella said, happy to see her friend, and trying not to groan at the thought of more carrots. "But I think we should skip this one. Let's get Bram from the lobby. I've got a werewolf story to tell you with a much better ending."

TURN THE PAGE FOR
A SNEAK PEEK OF

CHAPTER 1

The Beginning

THE Shiver-by-the-Sea Community Pool and Aquatic Center sat, silent and dark.

Except, that is, for the teenage boy wearing a bright blue polo shirt with STAFF printed across the back and a silver whistle around his neck.

He frowned at the algae-green gloppy mess in front of him. "No way anyone's going to be able to swim in that this weekend, no matter *what* I dump in there," he muttered.

His boss had left him a big bag of chemicals, a scooper, a bottle of liquid, and detailed instructions on a slip of paper.

"Two of this, one of that," the boy said, scooping. He walked around the edge of the pool, sprinkling the crystals across the top of the water. The harsh chemical smell tickled his nose.

Next, the bottle.

5 cups, read the instructions.

But there was no measuring cup with the bottle.

The boy glanced around, then checked the supply cabinet at the desk. Nothing. He eyed the scooper he'd used for the crystals. "This'll work, I guess."

The liquid dribbled a little as he poured, so he shifted the scooper over the pool.

One, two, three, four, five. The bottle was nearly empty.

"Hopefully, you'll be blue and beautiful in no time." His voice echoed in the big space.

The boy returned the chemicals to the supply cabinet.

Behind him, bubbles rose in the green, gloppy water.

He didn't notice. He closed and locked the door to the pool deck.

Thick, steamy fog gathered above the murky surface.

And then a webbed hand rose from the water and grabbed the edge.

PREPARE FOR MORE MONSTROUS FUN IN

ERIN DIONNE is the author of the Edgar Award-nominated *Moxie and the Art of Rule Breaking* as well as several other picture books and novels for middle grade and tween readers. She lives in Massachusetts with her family. Visit her online at ErinDionne.com.

JENN HARNEY is the author/illustrator of *Swim Swim Sink* and *Underwear!* and has illustrated many other beloved picture books and chapter books. She lives in Ohio with her family. Visit her online at JKHarney.blogspot.com.